FREE BOOKS

www.*forgottenbooks*.org

You can read literally <u>thousands</u> of books
for free at www.forgottenbooks.org

(please support us by visiting our web site)

Forgotten Books takes the uppermost care to preserve the entire content of the original book. However, this book has been generated from a scan of the original, and as such we cannot guarantee that it is free from errors or contains the full content of the original. But we try our best!

Truth may seem, but cannot be:
Beauty brag, but 'tis not she;
Truth and beauty buried be.

To this urn let those repair
That are either true or fair;
For these dead birds sigh a prayer.

Bacon

HIWA
A TALE OF ANCIENT HAWAII

EDMUND P. DOLE

HARPER & BROTHERS
NEW YORK AND
LONDON *MCM*

Copyright, 1900, by EDMUND P. DOLE.

All rights reserved.

TO

SANFORD BALLARD DOLE

CONTENTS

CHAPTER	PAGE
I. Ku is Avenged	1
II. The Vow	8
III. A Royal Marriage	11
IV. The Rescue of the Boat	17
V. Training a Warrior	28
VI. Hiwa's Visit	38
VII. Hiwa's Teachings	44
VIII. Manoa	51
IX. Kaanaana	66
X. "The Thunderbolt is Swifter than the Thunder"	71
XI. Over the Mountains	78
XII. The Battle	84
XIII. The Sacrifice	91
Glossary	99

HIWA
A TALE OF ANCIENT HAWAII

CHAPTER I

KU IS AVENGED

THE first glimmering of dawn rested on Waipio Valley. The *moi kane*, his great nobles and chief officers of state, his personal attendants, his guards, heralds, priests, diviners, bards, story-tellers, dancers, and buffoons, the whole *aialo*, even to the lowest menials of the court, slept the deep sleep that follows a night of heavy eating and heavier drinking. All slept except Aa, the terrible high-priest, and a few score men of his personal following. The royal city was silent.

It lay among surroundings both lovely and grand. The valley itself, only a few feet above sea-level and flat as a Western prairie, was, then as now, rich almost beyond exaggeration, and green with all edible products of the lowlands. It was thickly dotted with grass huts, for in those times, before the great wars and centuries before the white strangers came with their loathsome diseases that consumed flesh and bone, the population was dense.

The valley fronted on the open ocean, unobstructed by land for thousands of miles. On every other side it was shut in by rock walls from two to three thousand feet high. At the southwest extremity the Waipio River, cold from the mountain-side, clear and sparkling, fell six hundred feet to a narrow shelf of rock, and then, dropping a thousand feet more at a single plunge, suddenly became a sluggish stream, with a current hardly perceptible, winding its tortuous way to the sea. To the northwest were the Saw-Teeth of the Gods, wild and picturesque

KU IS AVENGED

verdure-clad mountains that to this day form impenetrable barriers between the plantations of Hamakua and North Kohala. To the southeast, stretching along the coast for a hundred miles, were the rich highlands of Hamakua, Hilo and Puna, rising, ever rising, as they recede from the sea until they reach the dizzy heights of Mauna Kea, and of Mauna Loa, where eternal winter wages intermittent war with rock fires from the bowels of the earth.

In the gray twilight of that morning, centuries ago, Eaeakai paddled his fishing-canoe down the Waipio River and up the coast, straight to the Saw-Teeth of the Gods. In the early morning there was good fishing opposite those stupendous cliffs, and Eaeakai had taken to himself a buxom *wahine*, who could not live on love alone any more than if she were a *haole* bride, but had to have her fish and poi. He was also in daily expectation of another responsibility. Thus far there had always been fish and poi in his hut, for he was industrious and thrifty, rich for a landless freeman, *kanaka-wale*, as his *kaukehi* or single dug-out was the trimmest and swiftest on all the Windward Coast. Best of all, he was a happy man, for he was very much in love with his own wife. So he chanted a love *mele* as he bent to his work.

He had scarcely reached his fishing-ground and bated his turtle-shell hook when he heard a rustling sound overhead. As he looked up he caught glimpses through the dense foliage of a woman, in the garb of Eve, rapidly making her way down the steep declivity, regardless of the sharp thorns and terrible lava that cut and tore her hands and feet and body. Yet, in spite of her desperate haste, and at the peril of her life, she firmly clutched and carefully guarded from rock and thorn the *mamo* which royalty alone might wear and live.

Eacakai gazed for a moment, dumb and motionless with amazement. Then he flung himself upon his face, crying, "*E moe o! E moe o! Hiwa, Moi Wahine!*"

Hiwa gave command before she reached the bottom of the cliff—"Fisherman, bring me the boat! *Wiki wiki!* Quick!"

Kneeling in his canoe, Eacakai paddled

KU IS AVENGED

to the shore and prostrated himself with his face to the ground, for well he knew that by Hawaiian law it was death for a common man like him to stand in the presence or in the shadow of Hiwa, *alii-niaupio, tabu moi wahine,* goddess-queen.

She sprang into the canoe, seized the paddle, and sped up the coast.

Eaeakai lay grovelling on the ground until she was a goodly distance from him. Then he sat up and began to realize that probably he was ruined. His boat, which made him the envy of fishermen for fifty miles around, and upon which he had spent months of patient toil, was gone. It was his pride, his wealth, his livelihood. Hiwa was fleeing from enemies. He could expect no reward if she should escape and return in triumph, for he was beneath her notice; but, if she should be overtaken and slain, the service he had rendered her would not be forgiven. The boat would tell the story, and he would be hunted down and killed or offered a sacrifice to the gods.

Presently, as he turned his eyes in the direction of his home, he saw a great war canoe approaching. He hid behind a rock and watched it. He counted twenty-six warriors at the paddles, and recognized Aa, the high-priest, commanding them. They had caught sight of Hiwa, and were doing their utmost to overtake her.

Eaeakai knew that an heir to the throne was expected. Who in all the land did not? "If it were not for her condition," he said to himself, "she might give them a long chase; but the end would be the same."

Her enemies rapidly gained on her, although she handled the paddle with marvelous strength and skill, and she seemed to have no chance of escape. Suddenly she plunged into the water and disappeared.

Her pursuers hastened to the spot. One of them reached out to save the boat, a chattel of great value to a Hawaiian; but the fanatical high-priest interposed. "Let it dash itself to pieces on the rocks!" he exclaimed. "It is accursed! *Tabu!*"

The shore at that point was a traverse section of one of the huge Saw-Teeth, rising from deep water nearly perpendicularly two thousand feet into the air. No living creat-

KU IS AVENGED

ure, save some insect or reptile that clings to the bare face of a rock, could obtain a foothold there. Hiwa was not a lizard to cling to that cliff, and if she were, she would be in plain sight. Neither was she a bird to soar above and beyond it. She was not a fish; if still alive, she must come to the surface. After watching for her long and anxiously, they discovered a few drops of blood. A sharp fin above the waves, slowly moving seaward, afforded a ready explanation.

The high-priest's face lighted with savage triumph as he cried: "Ukanipo, the Shark-God, hath her! Ku is avenged!"

So thought Eacakai. "Black death hangs over me!" he wailed. "Lilii will have no *kane* to bring her fish and poi and the little *keike* will be fatherless from its birth!"

The story of the death of Hiwa and of the unborn heir to the throne spread from lip to lip through the nation, and all men believed it and said, "Ukanipo, the Shark-God, hath her! Ku is avenged!" And a great fear fell upon them, the fear of Aa, the terrible high-priest of Ku.

CHAPTER II

THE VOW

A WOMAN lay on the ground. She was about twenty years of age, of regal stature; for among ancient Hawaiians men and women of kingly stock were gigantic, fully six feet in height, with broad shoulders, deep, full bust, and huge hips and limbs that indicated great vitality and enormous strength. Yet her figure, from the mighty neck to the delicately shaped feet, was so graceful in its outlines, so perfect a type of beauty in a giantess, that it would have been a joy to Phydias. Her face was full of intelligence, of firmness, of daring, and of pride; full also of passion, of tenderness, and of love. It was both strong and beautiful. Her head was massive and noble, like her body, and was crowned with a glory of jet-black hair reaching to her hips.

There was no clothing, not even an ornament, on her person. Her soft, delicate, satiny skin told of luxurious living. Exposure and pain and hardship were plainly new to her, and the *mamo*, which lay beside her, wet with the brine of the sea, was evidence that her rank among her people was like that of the immortal gods. Her hands and feet and arms and legs and thighs and body were bleeding, terribly cut and torn.

She endured her wounds and the pangs of maternity without a groan, her eyes resting meanwhile on the wall of rock, two thousand feet high, that encircled her. A rivulet, flowing from the mountain above, fell over the stupendous precipice, and the wind, eddying round and round in the enormous pit, the crater of an extinct volcano, spread out the water into a sheet of silvery spray like a vast bridal veil. The sun was now approaching meridian, and its rays, falling upon the spray, formed a brilliant rainbow, spanning the birth-scene.

As soon as the child was born the mother

clasped it in her arms and exultantly cried, "He shall sit on the throne of his fathers, for the rainbow covered him! Thus *mois* are born!"

Then she kneeled upon the ground and stretched forth her arms in prayer—"Eternal Ku, thou who bearest sway over gods and *mois* as over common men, hear this my vow! I have sinned, and my life is forfit; but the child is sinless, and if I die now he will perish. Spare me to him till he can hurl the spears and lead the chiefs in battle for his throne, and I will offer thee such priceless sacrifice as never yet was slain before a god, for I, the goddess-queen, with my own royal hand will shed my sacred blood to thee."

As she ceased a peal of thunder came from the mountains.

"Eternal Ku," she exclaimed, "thou hast heard and answered, and although I die, my child shall yet be *moi*, the mightiest of his line! His name is Aclani, The Pledge from Heaven."

CHAPTER III

A ROYAL MARRIAGE

"HIWA," said Papaakahi, The Mighty, not long before his death and about two years prior to the events already narrated, "you have grown to be a woman. It is time for you to marry."

"Yes, father," Hiwa replied, "it is time for me to marry."

"Traditions have come down to us from the beginning," continued Papaakahi, "that beyond the great ocean are many and strange lands, *kahiki*, and men with white skins, who are wise and powerful as gods. There may be a man in these foreign lands worthy to marry you; but, if there is, he cannot come to you, neither can you go to him. Our god, Lono, dwells there, and some time, ages hence perhaps, he will return and tell us of these things; but now we know nothing of them. There are only three men in the world we know about whose blood is fit to mate with yours. I am too old to marry you. Your uncle, Aa, shall not. There is no one else but your brother, Ii."

"But, father," pleaded Hiwa, "I do not love Ii."

"That is a small matter," said Papaakahi.

"But, father, I love Kaanaana, and he loves me. Why cannot I marry him?"

"He is not of the blood of Wakea, and Papa, my child, he is not descended from the gods."

"Yet he is a mighty *konohiki*, father, a great noble, the greatest of your vassals, and of all the men in the land his blood is next to our own. Besides, he is young and handsome and strong, first in the games and bravest in war, and his spearmen won the bloody battle that made you The Mighty."

"Yes, Hiwa, he is all you say, and I love

him better than I love your drunken brother; but he is not of the blood of the gods. You must marry Ii."

Then, because Papaakahi's word was the law of the land, which not even Hiwa could question, and because she loathed marriage to her brother, and loved Kaanaana more than her own life, she went away by herself and wept bitterly. She spent many days in solitary places, weeping and longing to die.

Papaakahi cared little for his drunken son Ii, and loved Hiwa as the apple of his eye, and when he saw how she grieved, his heart was heavy; but his purpose remained fixed. So he went to her and spoke gently and said, "If you marry Kaanaana it will bring civil war and your death."

"Father, why civil war?"

"Because I am old and must soon be hidden in a cave, and your first-born son would come before any child of your brother's as heir to the kingdom. You know our law; the child takes the rank of its mother, instead of the rank of its father, for all men know its mother and no man knows its father.

You yourself take divine rank from your mother, who was my sister."

Hiwa shuddered, and made no reply.

"Your brother," continued Papaakahi, "spends his nights drinking awa, and his days in sleep. He will rule in name only. Your uncle will be the real *moi*. He hates Kaanaana, and, if you marry him and have an heir, he will raise the standard of revolt as soon as I am dead."

"Then let spears settle it!" cried Hiwa, with flashing eyes. "I do not fear death, and I love Kaanaana. I will fight by his side, and we will slay Aa and his army, for the spearmen of Kohala will follow where Kaanaana leads, and he is greatest of the warriors, and I am daughter of the gods."

"*Ao keike!*" exclaimed the old man. "But I fear the great high-priest would prevail, and I will not have my people butchered and my kingdom destroyed and my daughter slain. Yet I would reason with you rather than command. I married my sister because the ancient custom of our race put that duty upon me, she being the only woman of birth equal to mine; but we were not *lolo*, fools, to be unhappy about it, for I loved other women, and she loved other men. You can be a good girl and marry your brother without being cold to your lover, can't you, *keike?*"

But Hiwa refused to be comforted.

The next day Papaakahi went to her again and asked her, "My daughter, have you considered well?"

Hiwa's eyes were hard and dry, as she answered: "I have no choice. Thy word is as the word of Ku."

"It is well said!" exclaimed the old *moi*. "You are a good girl, wise and discreet. Ii shall be your husband, and Kaanaana your lover. I have always loved you above all others, and next to you I love Kaanaana, and would choose him for your husband if he were of the blood of the gods."

"Then, father," Hiwa cried, "if you love him and love me, let me marry him! I loathe the custom of our race! I want one man as both husband and lover! I had rather be Kaanaana's wife one hour and then die body and soul than to marry Ii and be goddess-queen forever!"

"Hiwa, *pau!* It is not fitting that a daughter of the gods should marry a man of mortal blood. It has been done and, out of my great love for you, I might consent to it even now if I could not foresee war and death. Nothing could save you but Aa's death. The gods, our ancestors, tell me to kill him. It is my unquestioned right, for I am *moi*, Lord of Life and Death; yet I cannot kill him — he is my only brother. Therefore, and that you may have a place to hide till he is dead, I will reveal to you the secret of the hidden crater and of the passage to it beneath the sea."

Then Papaakahi told Hiwa of the crater in the mountain and how to find the passage to it, a secret which no other person living knew.

So Hiwa married Ii, and not many months afterwards Papaakahi's bones were hidden in a cave. And so, too, when she fled for her life, she dived into the sea, and of all who watched her not one saw her rise again, and the whole nation believed that Ukanipo, the Shark-God, had taken her to himself.

CHAPTER IV

THE RESCUE OF THE BOAT

THE Hawaiian Islands, as all the world knows, are entirely of volcanic origin. The soil, whether red or black, that produces a hundred tons of sugar-cane and fourteen tons of sugar to the acre, is lava pulverized by the suns and rains of thousands of years. The coffee lands are lava, rotten, honey-combed, porous, to a degree still unpulverized, but far on the way to becoming so. And the recent flows show what every part of every island has been— first, an overflowing sea of boiling rock; then, when the rock-currents froze, weird, fantastic, utter desolation. In the mighty crater of *Haleakala* (The House of the Sun) are rock-billows as they stiffened unknown

HIWA

ages ago, rock-billows five hundred feet high. And smaller volcanoes, once active, now extinct, are almost numberless.

Hiwa's refuge was the crater of one of these small, extinct volcanoes. At some time a lake of boiling rock, perhaps a mile long and three-quarters of a mile wide and a thousand feet deep, forcing a subterranean exit to the sea, had disappeared, leaving a huge *puka*, a hole in the mountain, some two thousand feet deep. As the centuries came and went the surface rock gradually became soil of marvellous fertility. Birds, flying across, dropped seeds of vegetables, fruits, shrubs, and trees. The place became a wilderness of luxuriant vegetation. In moist, eternal summer food for a hundred mouths ripened every day in the year. Nor was Hiwa denied her accustomed food from the sea, as well as from the land. The *makai* or sea entrance to the passage was some three or four fathoms below the ebb and flow of the tide, but after a few rods its roof rose abruptly to a height of several hundred feet, and the passage itself broadened into a large cavern, its bottom

THE RESCUE OF THE BOAT

being a salt-water pool swarming with fish. And the mountain rivulet, after its wild leap of two thousand feet, lazily crawled along the bottom of the crater till it reached the pool.

So Hiwa and Aelani were safe from hunger and thirst. Nature provided a varied and abundant diet. They had no need of clothes, for the days were not hot nor the nights cold. They had no enemies to fear. No other human being knew of their refuge or dreamed of their existence. There were no wild beasts to attack them, no poisonous serpents, no snakes of any kind, no reptiles or insects that could seriously injure or annoy them. In that age even mosquitoes were unknown.

But Hiwa did not look to a safe and easy existence. She had devoted her life to a great purpose. She had become more than a woman, more than a mother. Her son was Aelani, The Pledge from Heaven. The rainbow had covered him at his birth, and Ku had answered her irrevocable vow with thunder from the mountains. Separated from her lover, exiled from the human race, consecrated to death on the altar of Ku, yet still *moi wahine*, believing herself goddess-born, and as far above mere mortals as we think ourselves above the brutes, her sole remaining object in life was to care for her child, to teach him the accomplishments, duties and prerogatives of a *moi*, to prepare the way for his return to his people, and then send him forth to battle for his throne.

Her first task was to secure the fisherman's boat.

It is said that a native woman on Kahlooawe kept appointments with her lover on Lanai, swimming to meet him one night and returning the next, the round trip being nearly six miles. Such stories are accepted without hesitation by people familiar with a race which still spends much of its time in the sea, and was practically amphibious until civilization changed its habits.

Although in swimming and diving Hiwa had proved herself a match for Kaanaana, the champion athlete of the nation, she knew she was undertaking a task dangerous even for her, if not impossible. Yet she felt that the boat was worth risking everything.

THE RESCUE OF THE BOAT

At break of the day following the birth of her child, having nursed him and tenderly laid him on a soft bed of ferns, in the shade of a big *koa* tree, she swam forth, armed with a sharp stick to protect herself from sharks. Sharks, however, were a matter of small concern; the danger lay in the fierce waves and terrible cliff.

She crossed the pool, dived through the *makai* entrance, and struck boldly out to reconnoitre. The boat, as she anticipated, had been left, a thing accursed, to drift where it would. She found it, together with the paddles, a couple of miles to leaward, wedged between two rocks. It was uninjured, but dangerously near frequented fishing-grounds, and there was no time to lose. After an hour of hard work she got it loose and paddled swiftly to windward. It was necessary to load it with small rocks, to make it nearer the specific gravity of water, so that it could be floated or sunk at will; but no stones could be had for half a mile on either side of the entrance to the crater. The bare, perpendicular cliff, rising from deep water, made it impossible to get them at a nearer point, and, when she had gotten them, the weight and unwieldy bulk of her prize made progress exceedingly slow and difficult. She struggled on for hours.

"My child," she muttered, "will need this boat before he can be *moi;* and *moi* he shall be, for what the Ruler of the Gods promises never fails!"

A huge shark attacked her. As he turned to bite she jabbed the stick into his eye, and he disappeared, leaving blood behind. It was a moment of extreme peril to her undertaking, for the incident, trifling as it was, came near causing her to lose the ballast from the boat.

At length she neared the entrance to the crater. The supreme test of fortune, courage, skill, and endurance, was at hand, for the waves pounded against the cliff with tremendous power, and the boat had to be sunk some four fathoms and steered through a narrow passage of jagged rocks, where the water sucked back and forth with frightful velocity.

"It is impossible for a mortal," Hiwa repeated to herself, "but I am daughter of the gods—and it must be done!"

THE RESCUE OF THE BOAT

For some time she lay quietly on her back, just outside the surf-line, recovering her strength and watching for her opportunity. When it came she sank to a depth of about twenty-five feet, taking the boat with her. Then the wave struck her and bore her towards the cliff with resistless power. She had to keep the boat right side up or the ballast would be lost. She had to guide it to the entrance, straight as a spear to a warrior's heart, or it would be dashed to pieces. She had to make the entrance herself or be hurled against the rock, mangled out of human shape. The passage was small, and certain death awaited her a single yard above or below or to the right or to the left.

Strength, skill, and fortune favored her, or, as she would have said, the will of almighty Ku. After two minutes of life and death struggle she entered the passage with her prize, escaping destruction by a hair's-breadth.

Then the wave receded, the waters pent up within poured back, and Hiwa felt herself being irresistibly sucked to the open sea. With the quickness of thought she took a turn of the rope around a projecting rock, and thus hung on until the out-going current had nearly spent its force.

But already she had been four minutes under water. The strain of intense action, the excitement of extreme peril, and the torture of long-suspended respiration passed away. The horrible, sickening green and white of the mad flood in which she was perishing became cultivated lowlands, rich fields, beautiful meadows, and waving forests before her eyes, and the wild surge and roar seemed the loved voice of Kaanaana, in whose arms she was falling asleep.

"This," she said to herself, longingly, "is the peace the gods send to their children!" Then the thought returned to her, "If I die the child will die also!"

Even as Death seized her, her unconquerable spirit flashed forth, and she tore herself from his grasp. Abandoning the boat for the moment, she made her way through the passage to the surface of the pool.

As her lungs filled with air, the sweet delirium of a water death vanished, and her whole body was racked with pain. But it

THE RESCUE OF THE BOAT

was no time to heed that, and, diving again, she caught the incoming flood and saved the boat. Then, staggering to the tree where her baby lay half famished, she gave it her breast and fainted.

Sleep followed the swoon, the long, deep sleep of utter exhaustion, and then, after many hours of death-like unconsciousness, came dreams. She dreamed that Kaanaana, lying beside her, with his arms twined around her, told her, between hot kisses, that Ii and Aa were dead, and that he, being of the next noblest blood, could now marry her.

As she uttered a cry of rapture, the dream changed. She saw her child and her lover dead at her feet, and her fierce uncle stood before her with a bloody spear in his hand.

The swiftly succeeding events of the past two days came back to her in visions more horrible than the reality: her sin against Ku, the doom hanging over her, the flight, the pursuit, the escape, the maternity, the irrevocable vow, and the rescue of the boat —all these facts, colored and intensified by the ghastly fancies that come to us only in dreams.

She awoke with a shiver. Her head throbbed. Every bone in her body ached. Every nerve was pain. Yet, for the moment, superstitious terror and the reaction of a noble but over-taxed spirit were far harder to bear.

Baby fingers and a plaintive wail of hunger aroused her, and, when the little *keike* was again fed and sleeping, she arose and went to the boat, a few steps away, to satisfy her bewildered senses that the day's work was not a dream.

It rested upon the beach of smooth, hard, white sand, the gift of the coral insect, a rare one, too, on the rock-bound, windward coast of Hawaii. Tiny waves murmured on the shore as softly as a mother's lullaby. The thunder of the ocean was muffled by a wall of eternal rock, and the mad rush and swirl of waters in the passage sounded but faintly from the furthermost recess of the cavern. Save for these distant sounds and the occasional splash of a fish, the silence of death reigned. All around were black walls, two thousand feet high, and overhead shone the moon and the stars.

THE RESCUE OF THE BOAT

The beauty and grandeur of the solitude appealed strongly to Hiwa, child of an impressionable and poetic race, and restored her to her wonted frame of mind.

"Eternal Ku," she cried, falling on her knees, "Ruler of Gods, from whom I am descended, and to whom I shall return, I have rescued this boat through thy help. In it my child shall learn to do such deeds as I have done this day. In it, when he is grown, he shall go to meet the chiefs who will follow him to victory. I thank thee, Ku, and, when the time comes, I will pay thee with my blood according to my vow, knowing that my son is Aelani, The Pledge from Heaven, and that he shall yet be *moi*, mightiest of his line!"

CHAPTER V

TRAINING A WARRIOR

IT was well for Hiwa and Aelani that a generous soil and a soft climate gave them food and warmth. The separation from her lover, the hardships of the escape, the lacerations inflicted by sharp lava and thorny jungles, the ordeal of motherhood, the rescuing of the boat, the grief and suffering, the bodily exhaustion and mental strain, concentrated in forty-eight hours, which Hiwa had undergone, would have killed any ordinary woman. And Hiwa, of iron constitution as she was, escaped a lingering death from fever, fatigue, and wounds almost as narrowly as a sudden one from violence. For many days she lay tossing on her bed of ferns, sore from head to foot, bruised and strained and torn, aching in all her bones, parched with thirst, at times wildly delirious. Yet, in her lucid moments, she managed to nurse her babe, and to pick wild fruits sufficient to keep herself from absolute starvation. For her child's sake she fought hard for life and won. Health and strength returned to her.

Then began an existence much like Robinson Crusoe's on his desert island, but without clothes, tools, or weapons. It was unlike Crusoe's also, in that it was cheered by mother-love, and inspired by a great purpose.

Although Hiwa had been served from infancy by chiefs and chiefesses, she now did a slave's work with willing hands. She gathered grasses and made a hut—ample shelter from the rains. She plaited *tapa* and wrapped the royal *mamo* in it, and covered and sealed it with a coating of gums, and over all with a coating of coral sand, so that moths could not get at it or bees bore it or mice gnaw it, and she layed it away in a secret place. She also plaited *tapa* mats for beds and coverlets, and *tapa* garments for herself.

Among the first things she did, she chose a hiding-place in the cavern for the boat, and plaited a great quantity of matting, and collected a great quantity of gums, and covered the boat and sealed it up, as she had sealed up the *mamo*, that it might be perfectly preserved until Aelani should have need of it. The sealing of the boat was the work of three months.

Fire was a prime necessity. She had great difficulty in getting it, although she was acquainted with the only method known to her people, and had seen the thing done many times. Rapidly and with all her strength she rubbed a pointed stick in a groove, made in another stick of the *hau* tree, until at last the fine combustible powder in the end of the groove ignited. Then she fanned it to a flame, feeding it with dry leaves and little pieces of wood. During all her stay in the crater she never once allowed it to go out.

She made fish-hooks from shells, filing them down with a sharp stone, and braided lines and nets from the fibre of the *olona*. A few minutes' work each morning supplied her with fishes for the day. Sometimes she cooked them in *ti* leaves, but more frequently ate them raw, as the most refined people in the Hawaiian Islands do to this day—people of pure white as well as native blood. Some varieties of fish are considered great delicacies raw. The *malihini* (newcomer) marvels to see ladies and gentlemen who would grace any society in Europe or America eating fish raw; but he eats oysters raw.

Fish and *poi* are the Hawaiian staff of life. *Poi* is made from *taro*, one of the most digestible and nutritious of vegetables. Fortunately for the exiles, *taro* grew abundantly along the swampy borders of the stream. Hiwa baked it under ground, on hot rocks, and mashed it with a stone, and kneaded and pounded it until it became a soft dough, and mixed it with water and left it to ferment. Then it was *poi*, which little Aelani learned to eat almost as soon as his mother's milk. In that barbarous age, as now, making *poi* was considered too severe work for women, even for female slaves, and no chief had condescended to it; yet the goddess-queen bent her back to the task, meanwhile chanting to her child ancient *meles* that commemorated the glories of his ancestors for forty generations.

They were by no means confined to fish and *poi*. Baked bread-fruit, pounded up and mixed with milk of cocoanuts and juice of sugar-cane and berries, made a luscious dish closely approaching a civilized pudding. Any quantity of fruit was to be had for the picking, and Hiwa often succeeded in snaring wild geese, rich and fat from their diet of berries, and ducks that visited the pool.

Before Aelani was six months old he added to his diet of mother's milk and *poi* large yellow *ohias* and delicious berries, the *ohelo*, the *poha*, and the *akala*, sweetened with juice of sugar-cane. At the end of his first year he toddled down to the beach and swallowed the tiny fishes his mother gave him, their tails wiggling as they disappeared. At the end of his third year he swam like a fish himself, and felt as much at home in the water as out of it. And so, never seeing a human form or hearing a human voice save his mother's and his own, he grew to be a strong, supple, active boy, of brave spirit and of thoughtful, inquiring mind.

In time there was a work-shop under the shade of the great *koa* tree, and tools—shells of all sizes and shapes, sharp stones that served for knives, and rough stones that served for saws and files—and coral sand for polishing. Sticks and pieces of wood, heavy and hard like iron, were selected with anxious care, and were cut and fashioned with infinite labor. Hiwa worked patiently with the tools Nature gave her week after week, and at length that task was finished—the complete arms of a warrior of sizes adapted to a boy—a sling woven from his mother's hair, long spears, *pololu*, short spears, *ihe*, a war-club, *newa*, and a feather helmet, but not of the *mamo*, the *oo*, or the *iiwi*, for these were unattainable. There were also blunted darts, and circular, highly-polished disks of stone, swelling with a slight convexity from the edge to the centre, such as warriors used in athletic games.

Then a training, already begun, was patiently continued month after month and year after year. For two hours or more each day mother and son bowled the disks and fought sham battles. The teacher was intelligent and exacting. The pupil was apt. He was scarcely more than half grown when he could bring down a flying bird with his sling, and, while running at full speed, could hurl spear after spear at a hair's-breadth and not miss. He could catch spears faster than they could be thrown at him; he could parry them; he could avoid them, twisting his body like a flash of lightning. He could hurl the disks farther and straighter, run faster, leap higher, and stay under water longer than Hiwa, although in training him she had equally trained herself. She had been familiar with such things from childhood, and knew that in these warlike feats her boy already excelled all men except Kaanaana. He was also immensely strong for his years, and gave promise of gigantic stature.

He fought his first battle when he was eleven. He was sitting, as he had been taught to do, on a rock at the bottom of the pool spearing fish, when his mother dived down and hastily beckoned him to the surface.

TRAINING A WARRIOR

"It is a shark," she said as soon as their heads were above water. "I am going to kill him."

A man-eating monster eighteen feet long was swimming leisurely about, carrying terror to smaller fishes that had thus far found the pool a safe refuge from sharks, and had accordingly congregated in large numbers. It was the first fish larger than an *ulua* that Aelani had ever seen.

"Let me kill him!" he eagerly cried, catching hold of the stick, sharpened at both ends, which Hiwa held in her hands.

For a moment, as it seemed to Hiwa, her heart stopped beating. The boy was a mere child, and, if he should become frightened and lose his wits at the critical instant, he would surely be bitten in twain. But there was no sign of fear in his face. His eyes shone, and his pulses throbbed with the joy of coming battle. Why should not he do it? He was a fish himself almost, with human intelligence. He knew the trick perfectly, for in the training, in which nothing a warrior should know was forgotten, he had been exercised in it many times, his

35

mother personating the shark. Even base-born men faced sharks without fear, and Aelani, though but a child, was *Aelani*, The Pledge from Heaven.

"He is born to great deeds," reflected Hiwa, "and must learn to do them. And there is no danger, for only the God of Sharks can swim before a child of Wakea and Papa."

Nevertheless, she armed herself with a spear and kept near him.

The boy swam quietly out to within a few fathoms of the shark, and then lay upon the water, almost motionless. The great fish, thinking he had an easy prey, approached slowly and turned to bite. As he did so a small hand, quick as lightning, thrust the stick between his jaws, and they closed over it, burying one sharp end in the roof of the mouth and the other through the great tongue into the lower jaw. The next instant, with the supple swiftness of an *ulua*, the child dived and glided away. His work was finished. He had only to keep beyond reach of the mighty tail threshing the water in death agony.

TRAINING A WARRIOR

The teeth were laid carefully aside for the war-club of man's estate, and the bones were preserved for fish-hooks and other domestic uses. Soon, however, there was a glut of sharks' teeth and bones, for the flesh, being cast into the pool, attracted other sharks, and these, slaughtered in turn, lured still others to a cannibal repast and a sudden demise. The pool swarmed with sharks, and furnished Aelani great sport. Of course, other fish became less plentiful. Yet there were enough.

CHAPTER VI

HIWA'S VISIT

A GREAT longing came upon Hiwa to see her lover once more, and to learn what was taking place in the kingdom. The royal city was only eight miles away, and a swim of that distance and back again was no great feat. Neither, as she thought, would such a visit be attended with much danger.

So one evening, leaving Aelani asleep, she armed herself with a short spear and swam up the coast to the Waipio River. She chanced to land close to a fisherman's hut. The night was warm, there being no breeze from the sea, and the fisherman and his wife and their girl baby were sleeping on a mat outside.

The fisherman was Eaeakai, whose boat Hiwa had taken. His testimony as an eye witness to her death had turned aside Aa's wrath and saved his life. It did not occur to Hiwa that she had wronged him in taking his boat. Neither had he so regarded it. It simply was his fate. No more do we think that we wrong bees when we take their honey, or beasts when we take their skins. We look upon them as creatures quite different from ourselves, and existing merely for our own needs and pleasures.

Hiwa glanced at the fisherman and at the woman and child sleeping beside him. The appearance of the latter arrested her attention. The child was about the age and size of Aelani, and her features were strikingly like his and very beautiful. As Hiwa looked at the mother she saw that she bore an equally close resemblance to herself. The family likeness was plain as day, the blood of Wakea and Papa through forty generations. Hiwa had heard of a fisher-girl of marvellous beauty, but had never before deigned, to notice her. This, then, must be that girl; for no other woman in all the land could be compared with Hiwa.

"Beyond a doubt," she murmured, "this is my half-sister! Papaakahi, The Mighty, had many loves. So had my mother; but, if this woman were my mother's child, she could not be a fisherman's wife."

So Hiwa, believing that the fisherman's wife was what her lowly condition indicated, a king's daughter but not a queen's, dismissed the matter from her mind as of no consequence, and passed on to the palace of Ii. It was not a single building, but, like the establishments of wealthy Hawaiians even to this day, a little village. The principal house or hall was raised on a stone embankment, a wooden framework thatched with grass. Around it were many smaller buildings, used for eating and sleeping purposes and storehouses and for servants, the whole being enclosed by a stone wall. Men in all stages of intoxication were around the palace. Sounds of drunken revelry came from within. Shouts and snatches of song told the story.

"It is," mused Hiwa, "as Papaakahi said

it would be. Ii worships only *awa*, and Aa rules the land. One squanders the wealth of the kingdom, and the other is grasping and cruel. The time may come, perhaps too soon, when the chiefs will be ready to fight against them both."

On this occasion the retainers of the court were too drunk to take note of passers-by, and they had become so habitually turbulent and lawless that honest people avoided that part of the town after nightfall. Hiwa, therefore, had no difficulty in making her way undiscovered to a distant camp. When she reached it, further progress was quite another matter, for, although peace reigned throughout the land, a considerable body of men slept on their arms, guarded by vigilant sentinels. But, under cover of the night, and taking advantage of every hummock and shrub, Hiwa noiselessly crawled to the entrance of the great grass house of the chief. She found it guarded by a man who had often admitted her in times past—a warrior, brave, trusty, and silent.

Emerging from the darkness, she stood before him with uplifted hand. Instantly he dropped prone on the ground with his face in the dust.

"Laamaikahiki," she said, in low, soft, solemn tones, "I am the Spirit of Hiwa, whom Ukanipo, the Shark God, took to himself. I have come from the other world to bless your master. Retire twenty fathoms." Laamaikahiki, without a word or a sign, with his face still in the dust, wriggled backwards like a huge worm. Hiwa entered the house.

Kaanaana lay sleeping on a mat, his sling, spears, and war-club beside him. Hiwa stood motionless for some moments, gazing upon him. Of the two master passions of her life she herself could not have told which was the stronger: love for the man sleeping before her eyes, or for her child sleeping in the hollow of the mountain.

"Oh," she murmured, "how I long to feel his arms about me and his kisses on my lips! Death with him is sweeter than life without him. He is my life. If I make myself known to him, he will leave all and follow me to the mountain, or muster his vassals and hurl that drunkard from the throne. It might have been! But now it cannot be, for my sin would bring the heavy wrath of Ku upon him. I am a thing accursed!"

She bent over him and lightly touched his forehead with her lips. He stirred, opened his eyes, for an instant looked wonderingly at her, and then, with a cry of joy, sprang up to clasp her in his arms.

The self-sacrifice of love held her to her purpose. Moving backward, she restrained him with a gesture.

"I am only Hiwa's spirit," she said. "You cannot touch me. Do not try. Yet I love you with all my being, as I loved you when I was flesh and blood. I am permitted to come to you this once from the other world to bless you. May Ku's eternal blessings rest upon you, my own, my only love!"

Then she vanished into the darkness.

The next morning Aelani awoke in his mother's arms, and his little body was wet with her tears.

CHAPTER VII

HIWA'S TEACHINGS

FEW queens on thrones or in exile — indeed, few merely rich women can command such leisure as Hiwa might have had. She had no social functions, no social duties. Even the question of dress scarcely presented itself. Occasionally, on wet days, she put on a *pau* of *tapa*, and Aelani, when he grew to be a large boy, often wore a *malo*, or girdle, around his loins, and sometimes a *kihei*, or mantle, over his shoulders. Frequently, however, mother and child were arrayed more sumptuously than Solomon in all his glory, for, after the charming custom of their race, they made wreaths of fragrant dark-green *maile* and many-colored wild flowers, and decked each other from head to foot. But this was recreation, not work. The physical comforts of existence were at hand for the taking, and Hiwa might have spent her days, as many of her people do, lazily floating in the water or lounging in the shade.

On the contrary, she was never idle. She felt that the few years given her to prepare her son for his future work and station should be improved to the utmost, for, as soon as he were grown, she could be no more with him, but must pass from the altar of Ku to the gods from whom she came. She believed that a great *moi* should be a god among men by his attainments and qualities of mind, as well as by birth, and she was well qualified to instruct Aolani in all the learning and accomplishments of her age and nation, for there was no seclusion of women among Hawaiians, and she had seen and heard much both at court and in camp.

She taught him the national dances, *hula-hula*. They were extremely graceful, expressing all emotions and passions. Some were noble; some, according to our standards, were vile. She taught him the sports and the games of chance and skill, at which it was customary to play for high stakes. She taught him to sing and to play the *ukeke*, a rude guitar, which she made from bamboo and *olona*.

She spent much time in teaching him the ancient *meles*, the unwritten literature of the nation, its epic and romantic poems and love songs, perpetuated from generation to generation by men set apart for that purpose, for in her father's reign — before a drunkard came to the throne — they were always chanted at feasts and at human sacrifices, and when the bones of great chiefs were hidden in caves, and she had learned them by heart.

Most carefully she taught him the etiquette of court, camp, and *heiau*, the observance due a *moi*, who might stand in his presence, who should remain kneeling, and who must lie prostrate with their faces in the dust. At the same time she strongly impressed upon him the firmness, self-control, dignity, and condescension which should grace a god among men.

She told him of the high chiefs and chief-

HIWA'S TEACHINGS

essess, the great landed nobility who held their possessions of the *moi*, and of the lesser chiefs who held of the great ones, substantially according to the Feudal System of Western Europe in the Middle Ages.

As he grew old enough to understand something of the work that was set for him to do, she talked much about the great men of the kingdom, of their power, resources, traits and peculiarities, and of how he might most surely win them to himself. She knew them well, for it had been the wise policy of her father to keep them most of the time at court under his own watchful eyes. More than of any one else she talked about Kaanaana.

"He is Lord of Kohala, and a mighty chief," she often said, "the greatest, noblest, bravest, and best in the land. He is your father, and I love him even as I love you, *keike*, and he loves me. When the time comes you will give him a token from me. Then he will proclaim you *moi*, and Ku will protect you both in the day of battle and give you the victory."

She told him of the gods. "There are

three great gods," she said—"Kane, Ku, and Lono. Kane is greatest of the gods, the almighty father and creator of heaven and earth; but he sleeps through the ages, and gives no heed to what is done among gods and men, and, therefore, they do not heed him. Lono is so gentle and kind that men are not afraid of him, and so they forget him. Ku is active, masterful, fierce, and cruel, and delights in wars and human sacrifices, and bends all things to his will, and rules alike among gods and men; so we worship Ku. Wakea, our ancestor, is a great god, and, next to Ku, bears sway over heaven and earth; and the *mois* of his blood, whose bones have been hidden in caves, from the beginning down to Papaakahi, The Mighty, are also great gods. There are lesser gods—Kanaloa, Kane's younger brother; Milu, God of the Lower World; Pele, the red-haired Goddess of Volcanoes; Kanehoalani, God of the Sky; Kanehulikoa, God of the Sea; Kukailimoke, God of War; Mokuhalii—whom we call Ukanipo—God of Sharks, and many others; and *kupuas*, or demi-gods, and *kini akua*, or elves. Ae *keike!* There are many gods, but there is no other god like Lono!"

"Tell me about him!" exclaimed Aelani.

"He came to us from heaven," said Hiwa, "many, many generations ago, in the form and likeness of a man, and he lived on earth, and his mission was love. He hated tears and wars and human sacrifices. He told men and women to be kind to each other as they would have others kind to them. He taught the people many things which would have made them wise and happy if they had remembered and practised them; but they forgot his good words after he was gone, for he went away beyond the great oceans. He will come back to us some time, but not now, and meantime Ku rules gods and men by fear alone."

Year after year, as they lay at noon under the shade of the great *koa* tree, or at night under the moon and the stars, Hiwa talked with Aelani about the rites and ceremonies of the priesthood, and the arts of *kahunas*, and the traditions of her people, about their customs and ways of living, about the birds and beasts and fishes, about the country she had seen, and the mountains and streams and ocean. Everything she knew that she thought might be useful to him when he should go out into the world she told him again and again, until all these things became fixed in his mind. She told him the story of her life and her love. But she said nothing to him of her sin against Ku, or of the time, so close at hand, when she must shed her own blood on Ku's altar.

She also told him much about women, and he often wondered if they were very different from his mother, for he imagined that, as she alone of all living women was goddess-born, she must be more beautiful than any other. As he grew older, without knowing why it was so, he yearned to meet a woman.

CHAPTER VIII

MANOA

HIWA repeated her visits to Waipio many times as the years went by. In her anxiety to know the condition of affairs she frequently ventured where she was likely to be seen and recognized. She knew that she had been recognized on several occasions. By day it might have cost her her life; but, appearing only at night, when spirits were supposed to be abroad, she was regarded, not as Hiwa in living flesh and blood, but as the spirit of Hiwa that Ukanipo had taken to himself. She justly trusted to the superstition of the people for safety, knowing that she had become an object of mortal terror.

Sixteen years had passed since her escape. Ii was rapidly nearing a drunkard's grave, or, more accurately, the time when his bones would be hidden in a cave, for *mois* were not buried in the ground like common men. Aa had become *moi* in all but name, and ruled with bloody and cruel hands. The masses groaned under his ruthless exactions. Many of the lesser chiefs had been assassinated or sacrificed on the altars of Ku, and their possessions confiscated. The great chiefs were becoming restive and alarmed. Yet who should take up arms against the Lord of Life and Death, vice-gerent of Ku? Ii and Aa were of the blood of the gods. Hiwa knew how matters stood, and believed the time for action would come soon if the great nobles understood they could have a leader of divine birth.

Aelani had not reached his seventeenth year—a mere smooth-water swimmer. The pool, swarming with sharks, was a fine training school for a boy of twelve; but the ocean was the only proper place for an athletic young man, big, powerful, destined for great deeds. Aelani had learned to love it in its varying moods, and most of all when it was stirred to wrath, when tempests raged and huge waves dashed against the cliffs and broke in spray two hundred feet high. Many a time, in calm and in storm, Hiwa and Aelani had sported together in the open sea, like the fish to which they were almost akin, but always with the greatest precautions against discovery, for the superstition which protected her might not protect him. Now the time was at hand when risks must be taken.

"*Keike*," said Hiwa, one evening, "we will go windward to-night and see your royal city."

They emerged from the water, at their journey's end, close to Eaeakai's hut. On this night also the fisherman and Lilii, his wife, and Manoa, their daughter, were sleeping outside. The girl — just past sixteen, which is three years older in the tropics than in the frozen north — was surpassingly beautiful, as her mother and Hiwa had been in the bloom of early womanhood. She lay in the moonlight, her lips half parted, smiling in her sleep, as if happy dreams were her guests. Her lustrous black hair, reaching in heavy masses half way to her feet, was her only covering. It was not shamelessness. Neither was it the innocence of a babe. It was Nature untainted and unpurified by what we call civilization.

The sensations of the young man who had never before seen a female face or form save his mother's may be imagined more easily than described. He stood gazing, like one in a trance.

"Well, *keike*," Hiwa observed with a peculiar smile, as he reluctantly followed her, "at last you have seen a woman! And perhaps it is time you should."

Avoiding the town, they made their way to the Kukuihaele side of the valley, and climbed to a height of about five hundred feet. It seemed to Aelani, as the valley lay spread before him, that he had already seen it many times, it had been described to him so well. To his right was the winding trail, the serpentine ladder, that led to the heights of Kukuihaele, forming the southern exit to the outer world, and beyond, stretching northwesterly, long lines of white surf glistened in the moonlight and thundered on the beach. To his left was the mighty southern wall, and, at its further end, the stupendous falls of the Waipio River, sixteen hundred feet high. Then the wall bent irregularly to the northwest, apparently extending to the Waimano side; but Aelani knew that the valley, for a dozen miles more, wound its way, a deep chasm in the mountains. He knew the stream that traversed it, joining the Waipio River near the sea. He knew the rocky defile leading to the southwest, by which an army might some time enter to make him *moi*. He knew it from vivid description, although he could not see it. Opposite, across the valley, the Waimano cliffs, which Hiwa sixteen years before had scaled in her flight, rose to an altitude of three thousand feet, and below them, in the midst of rich, green lowlands, lay the royal town. In the centre of the town, distinguished by its size, was the palace of the *moi*, and near it that of the high-priest. Scattered through the valley, and also distinguishable by their size and the clusters of huts about them, were the town residences of the great nobles. Kaanaana's was on the Kukuihaele side, not far from where Hiwa and Aelani stood. But it was empty. He and his retinue had long since withdrawn to his domains beyond the mountains of Hamakua.

The night was calm, and, as Hiwa was pointing out things to be carefully remembered, and the houses of the different chiefs, a wail arose which, spreading beyond the town, reached them even where they stood. It was the mournful *au-we*, passing from lip to lip, at first low, gradually swelling to loud, passionate shrieks, and then subsiding to weird, blood-curdling sobs. A few started it, then hundreds, then thousands took it up, and the mountains echoed with it—"*Au-we! Au-we! Au-we!*"

Hiwa's face lighted with a smile of joy, at once savage and sublime.

"That," she exclaimed, "is the wailing for a dead *moi*! The drunkard has gone! Our time has come!"

She stood for some minutes, rapidly forming plans of action.

"Follow the cliff to the beach," she said at last, "and wait for me at the mouth of the river. It may be an hour. It may be more."

"I should go with you," urged Aelani.

"*Keike*," she cried, "do as I bid you! The Spirit of Hiwa must appear at the wailing for the dead *moi* to make the hearts of Aa and the hearts of his followers like the white milk of cocoanuts, and the *moi* that shall be must not be seen in his royal city till he comes to it with the spearmen of Kohala at his back."

So Aelani followed the cliff to the sea and waited at the mouth of the river. But Hiwa crept through the rank vegetation of the rich *kuleanas* until she reached the river, and swam softly up stream under the shade of the overhanging bushes until she was close to the palace of the *moi*, and there she hid herself in a clump of trees, a point from which she could see and hear what was taking place.

She knew that, for the next three days, according to ancient usage, there would be no *moi*, and therefore no law. She knew the nameless horrors that accompanied the wailing for a dead *moi*, the drunkenness, the mutilations, the bestial excesses, the wild carnival of cruelty, indecency, and lust, and the wiping out of life-long grudges with fire and bloodshed.

But the weak and friendless were nothing to Aa. His followers were the beasts of prey who would revel in outrage and murder. Why should he restrain them? Yet Hiwa, in amazement, saw him send twenty picked men in the direction of the sea, and heard him mention the name of Manoa. It could hardly be to murder her. The time for murder would be hours later, when men were frenzied with drink. But, if it were to save her from possibility of outrage, it was none too soon.

Hiwa dismissed it from her thoughts for the moment. Her first purpose was to fill the minds of Aa and his followers with superstitious terror. The great high-priest was as fanatical as he was bloody, and believed in the religion of which he was the official head. He bent over the body of his nephew, chanting:

"Ue, ue! Ua make kuu alii!
Ue, ue! Ua make kuu alii!"

And the assembled chiefs took up the refrain:

"Ue, ue! Ua make kuu alii!"

A voice, low and distinct, came from the river-bank, saying:

"Ue, ue! Ua make kuu alii!

Ae! Dead is the chief! The Spirit of Hiwa comes from the other world for the Spirit of Ii, Ruler of Land and Sea. And, lo! the Spirit of Hiwa prophesies, and her word is the word of a goddess who sees the things that have been and the things that shall be. Aa, The Bloody, shall be a mouse in the day of battle, and shall die a pig's death, and his bones shall not be hidden in a cave, but shall be put to open shame. And, behold! there shall come a *moi*, The Chosen of Gods. At his birth the rainbow covered him, and Ku thundered from the mountains. None shall be able to withstand him, for Ku shall go before him, and behind him the hills shall be black with spearmen."

Aa's cruel face was sallow with rage and terror, and blank amazement held the chiefs spell-bound. At length one of them, bolder or less superstitious than the rest, ventured to the river-bank whence the voice had come. The water flowed sluggishly and undisturbed. Far down towards the sea was a ripple that might have been made by a fish.

Hiwa swam under water for fifty yards, and then, having risen to breathe, took another long swim beneath the surface. So she kept on, alert and invisible. As she neared the hut of Eacakai, the fisherman, and raised her head, she heard loud voices, shrieks of terror, and a cry as of some one in death agony. She crept up under cover of the river-bank and looked. Aa's men were dragging Lilii and Manoa away in the direction of the town, and Eacakai lay on the ground with a spear-thrust through his body.

Beneath caste and religion, which put an immeasurable gulf between them, Hiwa had a woman's heart. Besides, she remembered the fisherman had been the means of saving her life. Then she was beginning to think it possible that Lilii was her mother's as well as her father's daughter, and, if so, Manoa, being of the blood of the gods, was a fit mate for Aelani. As soon, therefore, as Aa's men were at a safe distance she went to Eaeakai and bent over him. But the moment he saw her he shrank from her in fear, and, with his last remaining strength, turned and buried his face in the dust.

"I do not want to live," he moaned, "for they have taken the joy of my heart and the life of my life. But why do you come—a vision to me—oh, goddess? Leave me to die alone!"

Then Hiwa spoke very gently to him, and tears stood in her eyes. "You shall die in peace," she said, "and your body shall be buried in the ground as becomes your degree. I cannot save your life, my poor fellow; I would if I could. It may not be given me to rescue those you love, but this much I promise you, I will try."

"Goddess," murmured the dying man, "I thank you with my face in the dust."

"One thing more!" cried Hiwa, and her voice grew stern, and her eyes flashed. "I swear to you that Aa, who did this thing, shall die a pig's death, and his bones shall not be hidden in a cave, but shall be put to open shame!"

Again the fisherman murmured his thanks.

"But why did he take them?" inquired Hiwa, her suspicion becoming almost a conviction that he had a deeper motive than the mere possession of a young and beautiful woman.

"I do not know," replied Eaeakai.

"Who is your wife? Who was her mother?" Hiwa demanded, for she saw that the man's life was fast ebbing away.

"I do not know," he feebly answered. "She was exposed and adopted, picked up, a new-born babe, the very day the great goddess who now speaks to me was born."

"Who found her? Who picked her up?"

Eaeakai tried to answer, but the death rattle was in his throat, a convulsive shudder ran through his frame, and, with his face still in the dust, he died.

Hiwa swam to the mouth of the river, where she found Aelani waiting. In a few words she told him what had happened, but not what the dying man had said. She had never before seen him so deeply moved. Although time pressed and a kingdom was at stake, they returned and buried the fisherman according to his degree, as had been promised.

As they swam home in the small hours of the morning, Hiwa pondered on many things, not least on the mystery of the fisherman's wife and daughter. She remembered that Lolo, the court jester, once asked her if she had seen her twin sister, and, when she repeated the saying, that her mother laughed and said it was only the quip of a fool; but, never hearing of it again, she did not believe it, although she knew the custom of her people, and also that Lolo died that night of a broken head.

More kittens are drowned than grow up, yet there is no dearth of cats. Infanticide was regarded in much the same way by the ancient Hawaiians. No woman was thought worse of on account of killing her babies, and a large percentage of new-born children were exposed to perish, or to be picked up and adopted, as chance might direct. Hiwa and Lilii, therefore, might be twin sisters, and it might have been thought that twin princesses, too divine to marry mortal men, would cause state embarrassments. The more Hiwa thought it over the more probable it seemed.

"Aa," she mused, "is old and not fond of women. He would not do this thing for the girl's youth and beauty. Ambition is his ruling passion, and now that Ii is dead it blazes up in a fierce flame. If he knows, as I believe, that they are my mother's child and grandchild, he means to kill one to cut off all possibility of rival heirs to the throne, and to marry the other. That is why he seized them the moment my brother was dead. If the girl is Aelani's cousin on my mother's side, the boy shall have her for his wife in spite of Aa, for her blood is divine."

So Hiwa, pondering on these things, and planning for the future, swam silently homeward. Aelani swam in silence by her side. A new inspiration had come to him. The master passion of love had taken a mighty hold on him. Heretofore he had been a patient and painstaking pupil—not because he greatly cared to be a *moi*, but because he loved his mother. Now the pathway to the throne was his only pathway to Manoa.

CHAPTER IX

KAANAANA

WHEN Hiwa returned from Waipio, and had satisfied the cravings of hunger, she lay down and slept until the shades of evening fell. She slept fourteen hours, and then arose and ate again, that she might have strength for her journey. She put on a *pau* of *tapa*, for it was not seemly for her to go to the camp of a great chief unclothed. Then she embraced Aelani and kissed him, and taking a short spear to protect herself from sharks, swam forth into the night.

She swam northwesterly, down the coast—that is, with the prevailing winds—until she came to Niulii, which is just beyond the mountains of Hamakua and on the edge of Kohala. It was only four or five miles; but when she reached Niulii she knew not whether her journey was nearly ended or only just begun, for Kaanaana, not leaving the control of his affairs to others, travelled much within his domains. So she went to a hut and wakened a fisherman, who told her that the Lord of Kohala was camped not a mile away with a hundred fighting men. The fisherman readily undertook to guide her, for there seemed good prospect of reward, and also because her bearing proclaimed her a person of high degree, and it was death to refuse a service to man or woman of the rank of high-chief.

When she drew near to the camp she dismissed him, telling him to return on the third day for a recompense. Then she walked boldly up to a sentinel, who challenged her. But when he saw her face, he fell grovelling in the dust, and she said to him, "I am the Spirit of Hiwa. Thy master hath need of me." So she passed on, and the sentinel told it to others, and it spread through the camp, and all wondered what this great sign portended, for Ii's death was not yet known in Kohala.

HIWA

When Hiwa came to the house where Kaanaana slept alone, she found it guarded, as of old, by Laamaikahiki. He also fell grovelling in the dust, and crawled away at her command. Then she entered the house and lay down on Kaanaana's mat, and put her arms around him and kissed his lips and cried for joy. So she awoke him. At first he thought it was a dream or a heavenly vision; but when he found that she was indeed Hiwa in living flesh and blood, his happiness was unbounded, for he had mourned her as dead sixteen years, and had loved no other woman. And she lay in his arms all night, and told him everything that had happened, save only her sin against Ku and her vow. She did not tell him of the sin lest he should loathe her, or of the vow, for she knew it would break his heart.

When morning came Kaanaana commanded Laamaikahiki to wait on Hiwa, for, although Laamaikahiki was no longer lord of broad lands, he was of ancient and noble blood, and was devoted to his chief, and had the golden gift of a silent tongue; therefore Kaanaana chose him before all others for the honor of serving the goddess-queen. But Kaanaana, having ordered yellow stain, with his own hands stained Hiwa's garment the royal color. Having done this, he assembled his vassals and fighting men, all that were with him, and they stood, rank by rank, with spears in their hands, in front of the house, and their lord stood at their head.

Hiwa put on her garment, and went out and stood before them. And Kaanaana fell upon his knees, and bowed his head to the ground, and kissed her feet. The lesser chiefs, also, fell upon their knees, and bowed their heads to the earth, and those of low degree lay prostrate in the dust.

Then Hiwa said: "I am Hiwa, *Moi Wahine*, daughter of Papaakahi, The Mighty, Child of the Gods. When Aa, the wicked high-priest, pursued me to kill me, Ukanipo, the God of the Sharks, rescued me and carried me to a cavern in the mountains known only to himself. There I gave birth to a son, who is also the son of Kaanaana, your high-chief. The rainbow covered him at his birth, and Ku thundered from the mountains. His name is Aclani, The Pledge from Heaven,

The Chosen of the Gods. He is now rightful *moi kane*, for Ii is dead. He shall be mightiest of his line, and none shall be able to withstand him, for, in the day of battle, Ku shall go before him, and behind him the hills shall be black with spearmen."

Then Kaanaana answered: "Hiwa, *Moi Wahine*, daughter of Papaakahi, The Mighty, Child of the Gods, it is thou who hast said it. No man can doubt that Ukanipo, the God of Sharks, rescued thee, and carried thee to a cavern in the mountains known only to himself. Nor is it passing strange, for we all do know from the ancient *meles*, which have come to us from many generations of wise men, that Ukanipo often did such things in olden times. Ii being dead, thy son and mine is *moi kane*. His word is as the word of Ku. The spearmen of Kohala await his commands."

CHAPTER X

"THE THUNDERBOLT IS SWIFTER THAN THUNDER"

HIWA wished to make the secret entrance to the crater known to Kaanaana, and they both thought it should not be disclosed to any one else. So he accompanied her on her return, the night after her arrival, having first given orders that no one should follow them under pain of death.

They found Aelani awake. "*Keiki,*" said Hiwa, "this is your father. His spearmen await your commands."

Then Kaanaana kneeled before his son and kissed his feet. But Aelani raised him from the ground and put his arms about him and kissed him.

"My father," he said, "I love you because

my mother loves you better than her own life, and has talked to me about you every day since I was a little child. While the homage due the *moi* cannot be omitted in public, between us three I am not a god among men, but only your son."

Then Kaanaana embraced Aelani, and the two ate together, Hiwa sitting not far off, for it was contrary to the commands of Ku for men and women to eat together. After the *moi* and his father had eaten by themselves, and Hiwa had eaten by herself, Aelani slept in the grass hut, and Hiwa and Kaanaana slept under the great *koa* tree, for the moon had gone behind the mountains, and it was not safe to attempt taking the fisherman's boat through the passage in pitchy darkness.

It was easy, however, in daylight, for there were three of them and a calm sea. So they set forth early in the morning and went to Niulii. But there were fishermen from Waipio fishing opposite the cliff who fled home in terror, and reported that they had seen the Spirit of Hiwa issuing from the depths of the sea, and with her the Lord of Kohala and a young man whom they knew

"SWIFTER THAN THUNDER"

not, and that the three had a boat provided by the God of the Ocean, exceeding light and swift, in which they sped down the coast. The tale was taken straightway to Aa, and it greatly troubled him.

Meanwhile rumors had gone forth through all of Kohala round about Niulii, and, when Aelani arrived, wearing the royal *mamo*, thousands of people had assembled to do him homage. They were cooking a great feast for him in an *umu* or underground oven of hot stones — fatted dog and pig which he had never tasted, and *taro* and bread-fruit, and many kinds of *lawalu* fish. Also they had prepared many kinds of delicate raw fish, flavored with *kukui* nuts, and crabs and shrimps and mosses. There were also fruits and berries, both from the lowlands and from the mountains. Neither was there any lack of *awa* that all might drink and be merry.

But Aelani, as soon as he had received the homage of the people, called a council of war, for time was precious, and the thought that Manoa was in the power of his enemy was like a hot coal in his breast.

It was only a dozen miles from Niulii to Waipio by water; but Kaanaana had not war canoes wherewith to fight Aa on the sea, neither had he canoes of any kind to carry a sufficient force of fighting men. Therefore, an attack on the coast side would have been madness; but the Saw-Teeth were impassable, and the trail around them was long and difficult.

"My Lord of Kohala," inquired Aelani, "how many spearmen can you have at daylight to-morrow morning, with provisions to cross the mountains?"

"Not more than eight hundred," replied Kaanaana. "But I will have five thousand on the fourth day."

"Eight hundred to-morrow," said Aelani, "are better than five thousand on the fourth day. If Aa depends on Kaaahu, Lord of Honokaa, he leans on a fern that will sway back and forth as the wind blows. Yet the *ahupuaa* of Honokaa is the nearest of the great lordships, and the only one from which Aa can muster many spears before the fourth day. We should strike before any of the great chiefs can come to his help from the

"SWIFTER THAN THUNDER"

south, for we are few at best, and only a small part of the kingdom."

Kaanaana fell upon his knees and bowed his head to the ground. "Child of the gods," he said, "shall I speak my *manao?*"

"Rise and speak!" exclaimed Aelani. "Thou art the greatest and wisest of my nobles. Thy *moi* will ever listen to thy *manao.*"

"My *manao* is that the great chiefs will not hasten from the south. They do not love Aa, and will stand aloof if they dare, or side with us if we seem the stronger. Moreover, Aa has twelve hundred fighting men at Waipio, and Kaaahu can bring him a thousand more before we can get there. Our way is over steep and difficult mountains, among sharp rocks and utter desolation, where mice would die of hunger and thirst, and even lizards cannot live. Our spearmen, exhausted with the journey, must fight men strong with rest and sleep. If we start tomorrow, we shall also be greatly outnumbered, and if we lose the battle not one of us will ever return. If we wait till the fourth day, and only one or two chiefs come against us from the south, we can meet Aa with equal numbers. Yet it shall be as the *moi kane* says. His word is as the word of Ku."

"Kaanaana, Lord of Kohala," said Aelani, "I thank thee for honest counsel, and I would also have the lesser chiefs freely speak their *manao*."

Thereupon the lesser chiefs fell upon their knees and bowed their heads to the earth, and the foremost of them spoke for all and said: "The way is most difficult, and eight hundred spearmen are not many, yet what the Child of the Gods says that we will do, whether it be life or death. His word is as the word of Ku."

Then Hiwa spoke, as was her right in the royal councils, being equal in birth and rank to the *moi kane* himself, although not in power. And she said: "The Lord of Kohala is the wisest and greatest of the nobles. He and the lesser chiefs have spoken well; but fear now dwells in the heart of Aa and in the hearts of his followers. My *manao* is to strike before it passeth away, that the hearts of the chiefs in the south may also become like white wax of cocoanuts, and that they may turn from him in the beginning."

"As Hiwa hath said, so be it!" exclaimed Aelani. "We march to-morrow at break of day. The thunderbolt is swifter than the thunder."

Instantly fast runners were sent forth to summon the spearmen and get supplies of food. Then Aelani ate and drank, and the chiefs were merry, but Aelani's merriment was feigned, for he greatly feared for Manoa's safety, and was impatient for battle because she was in the power of his enemy.

CHAPTER XI

OVER THE MOUNTAINS

EIGHT hundred and nineteen men, armed and provisioned, were on hand at daybreak the next morning. Aelani made a stirring speech, telling them that Ii was dead, and that Aa was preparing to invade Kohala to slaughter all the men and give their wives and *kuleanas* to strangers. And Kaanaana told them of their new *moi*, rainbow-covered and heaven-born.

The spearmen raised a great shout and cried: "His word is as the word of Ku, and we will follow Kaanaana, our high-chief, where spears are thickest, even unto death!"

Hiwa accompanied them. When Kaanaana privately remonstrated, she replied: "Hardships and hunger and thirst are heaven with you, my lover, and so are wounds and death; but without you, all the world is hell to me. What mortal man can do and suffer, that surely can I, daughter of the gods. Moreover, if the chiefs do not see me, whom they know, they will say that Aelani, whom they do not know, is but an impostor. My love, I must go with you."

So she went to the war, and was ever by Kaanaana's side, save at meals, which their religion forbade. Although Ii was now dead, Kaanaana did not seek to be Hiwa's husband, for he loved her too unselfishly to wish her to demean herself, being goddess-born, by marriage to a mortal. And she did not propose marriage to him, which would have been her place by custom, she being the higher of rank, because she would not involve him in the wrath of Ku. She counted the coming days of suffering and battle as precious—every moment, because they were spent with him, for she knew that as soon as they were over she must leave him and die on the altar of Ku.

Aelani marched with elastic steps at

the head of his little army. He ate plain fish and *poi* like the meanest soldier, drank tepid but precious water as sparingly, and bore the withering midday heat of the lava-flows and the cold night winds of the mountains as if they were the eternal June of the lowlands. So also did Hiwa and Kaanaana, knowing that where leaders share all hardships cheerfully their followers do not lose heart.

On the evening of the second day they had crossed the mountains, and were within half a dozen miles of Waipio. They could not take the enemy entirely unawares, for those fleeing before them had carried the news. Nor were they in a condition to fight that night, for they were utterly exhausted. Nearly fifty had dropped of fatigue by the way, and three, falling over a precipice, had been dashed to pieces on the rocks a thousand feet below. The little army camped in a wood hard by and slept till morning.

Hiwa slept two hours. Then she awoke Kaanaana with a kiss and said: "I have wakened you, my love, that you might not awake later and miss me from your side. I am going to the enemy. Our scouts, as you know, report the gleam of spears on the heights of Kukuihaele. It is Kaaahu and his thousand men come to the help of Aa. Our men are outnumbered three to one, and so worn out they can hardly stand. Some of them are dying of fatigue, and some have already died."

"And you, my love," interrupted Kaanaana, "will also die unless you sleep this night."

"No," replied Hiwa, "I shall not die of fatigue, nor yet of spear-thrust from mortal man. I shall live until our son is unquestioned *moi*. A goddess gave me life, and only through a god shall it be taken from me. My fate is unalterable. It is in the hands of Ku. *Pau!* My love, you know that your spearmen, exhausted as they are, cannot fight two thousand men. They will be slaughtered like swine in to-morrow's battle, and our cause will be lost unless I put fresh fear in the hearts of the enemy."

Kaanaana made no further objection, knowing that her words were true, and that, unless she succeeded in her mission, they must all die together. When she had gone, although his heart was heavy on her account, he turned over and slept soundly that he might have strength for the morrow's battle. So Hiwa went forth and descended the heights to the Waipio River, which, even at that distance from the sea, was then deep enough for swimming. The water and the change of motion greatly refreshed her bruised and bleeding feet and aching limbs. She passed the hostile sentinels, swimming noiselessly under water, and kept on down the river to the midst of Aa's army.

Then Aa's spearmen, sleeping on their arms, were awakened by a well-known voice proceeding from the water, and it said:— "Listen! The Spirit of Hiwa bids you save your lives. Why should you die? Behold, the rightful *moi kane*, *Aelani*, The Pledge from Heaven, The Chosen of the Gods, cometh to his own! Ku thundered at his birth, and the rainbow covered him; therefore none shall be able to stand before him. Yet he is just and merciful. He will slay those who are taken with arms in their hands, fighting against him. He will spare those who stand aloof. But Aa shall die a pig's death, and his bones shall be put to shame."

Then Hiwa swam down-stream under water so softly that not a splash was heard or a ripple seen, and an hour past midnight the same voice and words were heard on the heights of Kukuihaele.

At dawn Kaanaana awoke and looked upon Hiwa sleeping at his side. She was covered with blood, and great, ragged rents were torn in her flesh, for she had slipped and fallen while descending from the heights of Kukuihaele in the darkness of the night. Her eyes were sunken, her face was gaunt with toil and pain, and she slept like one dead. Kaanaana forbade all noise in that part of the camp, and made it silent as the grave, so that Hiwa might sleep until the men were ready to go forth to battle. Then he awoke her gently, and she arose and took her place beside him at the head of the warriors, armed as a warrior, and so she marched to the fight.

CHAPTER XII

THE BATTLE

A was brave as well as cruel. He did not doubt that Hiwa's spirit had appeared in his camp and on the heights of Kukuihaele; but, although it troubled him greatly, he hoped it was a lying spirit. Did not the whole nation know that the *moi wahine* had committed the unpardonable sin and had died from Ku's implacable wrath, which descends from parent to child even unto the third and fourth generation? How, then, could her claimant to the throne enjoy Ku's favor? And how could he be of the sacred race which the gods had sent from heaven to rule men? Yet Hiwa's spirit had thrice proclaimed him as heaven-born, The Chosen of Ku, and living witnesses had seen him and Hiwa and Kaanaana issue from the depths of the sea, where mortals unaided by the gods would have perished. Superstition balanced superstition. Men were afraid to support Aelani, and afraid to fight against him, lest the heavy wrath of Ku should fall upon them.

It was not so with the spearmen of Kohala. Kaanaana had always believed that Aa invented the story of Hiwa's sin as a pretext for hunting her to death, and what the highchief believed was accepted in his own domains without question. Had it not proved true? Was she not now with them in living flesh and blood? Was not the story of her rescue by Ukanipo, God of Sharks, reasonable and in accord with the sacred *meles* that had come down from the wise men of old? Most convincing of all, would Ku have permitted her to live if she had committed damning sin?

Before the spearmen of Kohala arrived, Aa succeeded in persuading most of his immediate followers, and also himself, that Hiwa was a lying spirit. He even won over Kaaahu, Lord of Honokaa, who was swaying between opposing opinions like a fern in the wind, and set him and his men in the front of battle, where they could not easily run away.

The old men, the women, and the children had collected in the *puuhonua*. This was a city of refuge corresponding to those of ancient Israel. These sanctuaries, some of them very large and with accomodations for many people, were scattered throughout the Hawaiian Islands. Their gates stood always open, and the vanquished warrior, the rebel, the red-handed murderer, the violator of *tabus*, the vilest criminal, or the bitterest enemy of the *moi* or of the priesthood, was safe when once within their sacred walls. There he offered thanks to the gods for his escape, and, after a few days, was free to depart under their protection. It is said that, in the latter part of the fifteenth century, long after the period of this story, Hakau, The Cruel, proposed to slaughter the followers of his half-brother, Umi, within the sanctuary, and was deterred by the threatening vengeance of the gods— incidentally, also, by his own death, and the complete triumph of Umi. Where did these people, so remote and isolated, get this and so many other of the customs described in the Jewish scriptures?

It was past noon when the conflict began —less than eight hundred tired men attacking twenty-two hundred fresh ones. But as the spearmen of Kohala advanced, amazement paralyzed the ranks opposing them. The *moi wahine,* or her spirit, marched in front, and beside her strode a youth, wearing the royal *mamo,* who was the living image of Papaakahi, The Mighty, in his younger days, but of more gigantic stature, and handsomer, and more regal in his bearing, than even that great conqueror.

Kaahu and his men, crying that the dead had come to life, and that Aelani must be The Chosen of the Gods, broke and fled without throwing a spear. They made their way with no great loss to the heights of Kukuihaele, and watched the battle in safety. But, in the confusion, Aa and his spearmen were forced back, and were hedged in with the cliffs of Kukuihaele at their left, and the river at their right, and the sea behind them. They could not run away, and, as they expected no quarter, they fought with desperation. The odds, too, seemed greatly in their favor, for they were picked warriors, many of them nobles, and were fresh, and far outnumbered their assailants.

But doubt and superstitious fear were with them, while the spearmen of Kohala were confident of victory, and forgot their weariness in the blood-frenzy of battle. Their *moi kane* was at their head, and beside him the *moi wahine*, and Kaanaana, their high-chief, the foremost warrior in the land. So, although they fell thick and fast before Aa's skilled spearmen, they pressed on and slew and slew and slew. The *moi kane* and the *moi wahine* and the Lord of Kohala, excelling all others in deeds of strength, and skill and valor, were ever in advance, their spears, dripping with blood, yet they received no hurt so that men said that Ku went before them. They continually strove to reach Aa and kill him, for his death would end the war; but his spearmen, knowing the rout and slaughter that would follow, protected him with dense ranks of spears.

Then Aelani did a marvellous thing, one

THE BATTLE

that was told in after ages, which no man could have done without long and patient training. He hurled a spear over the heads of Aa's men, fully seventy yards, so that it struck Aa below the waist and passed through his body. Aa fell, and his warriors, supposing that he was dead, became panic-stricken, and, being hemmed in by the cliffs and the sea and the river, were slaughtered without mercy.

Just as the fighting changed into a butchery, Aelani plunged into the river and swam across, and ran with all his speed towards Aa's palace. He had heard a shriek, and, looking that way, saw Manoa rush from the palace in the direction of his army, pursued by three men armed with spears. So he hastened to her rescue. As he drew near to the men, they flung their spears at him at the same moment. He evaded one of the spears, and caught the other two in his hands as he had been taught to do in his childhood. Then he flung the two spears back, killing two of the men with them, and the third he killed with a stone. Thus he saved Manoa's life.

The thing was the wickedness of Aa, for, knowing that Lilii and Manoa were of the divine blood of Wakea and Papa in the female line, he had commanded that they should be killed if the battle went against him, so that the victor might have no goddess-born wife. He had assigned the murder to the three men he trusted most, and they killed the mother before the daughter escaped.

The slaughter ended when darkness came. A few of Aa's men scaled the heights of Kukuihaele; a few swam out to sea and got away; a few score swam across the river and reached the *puuhonua* and were safe, but many more were speared in attempting it. The greater part perished. A fourth of Kaanaana's men perished also. In all more than a thousand men lay dead and dying on the field. The victorious survivors, worn out with marching and slaughter, sank on the ground beside them and slept until morning.

Hiwa and Kaanaana slept from dark till dawn; but the young *moi kane*, who had that day won his kingdom, lay awake many hours, and when sleep came to him he dreamed of love, and not of glory.

CHAPTER XIII

THE SACRIFICE

IN the morning after the battle word was brought to the palace that Aa had been found on the field still alive. Aelani commanded that he should be taken to the *heiau*, or temple, to be sacrificed, and that the spearmen should be assembled there to witness the sacred rites. So Aa was taken to the *heiau*, and awaited the coming of Aelani and Hiwa and Kaanaana and the spearmen of Kohala.

Then Aelani's servants put on him the great *mamo* that had been the state robe of *moi kanes* of the blood of Wakea and Papa time whereof the memory of man ran not to the contrary. It reached from his shoulders to his ankles, and enveloped his whole body.

It was made entirely of the yellow feathers of the *mamo*, and, as the *mamo* was a small bird, and lived in the mountains, and was wild and scarce, from being constantly hunted, and, moreover, had but few of the sacred feathers, the collection of feathers for that cloak had been the life-work of nine generations of hunters. Aelani also wore a helmet of the still more priceless feathers of the *oo*. The *niho palaoa* was on his neck, and in his hand he carried spears red with the blood of his enemies.

Hiwa wore a *mamo* like Aelani's, broad and long, extending to her foot, priceless as the crown jewels of England. Upon her head was a *lei*, or wreath of yellow *ilima* and dark-green *maile*, and, crowning all, a *lei* of the fluffy, yellow feathers of the *oo*, feathers worth many times their weight in gold. Kaanaana, too, was richly clad, as became a mighty high-chief. A cloak of yellow and red feathers, only less rare and costly than the *mamo*, covered him from head to foot, and a yellow and red helmet adorned his head.

Before they left the palace Hiwa embraced

THE SACRIFICE

Aelani and Kaanaana, kissing them and shedding tears, as if she were parting from them forever, so that they greatly wondered, not dreaming of what was in her mind. Then, when the chiefs had assembled—all who had the right to stand in presence of the *moi*—Hiwa made a signal that Kaanaana should kneel before her. So he kneeled before her, and she, in presence of them all, took the feather *lei* from her head and twined it around his helmet.

"Mighty *konohiki*," she said, "thou art greatest of the chiefs, noblest among men, my own and only love, the father of my child. Thy rank shall be above all other men not goddess-born, and, in token thereof, thou and the *konohikis* of thy line shall have the right to deck their helmets with the yellow feathers of the *oo* as long as the sun shines and water flows. I, Hiwa, daughter of the gods, have said it, and my son, The Chosen of Ku, confirms this royal honor."

The occasion of the sacrifice was a great one, for Aa was of the blood of Wakea and Papa. Never before in the solemn and bloody rites of consecrating a new *moi* had such an offering been made to Ku. The *heiau* was an immense, irregular, stone parallelogram, open to the sky. The interior was divided into terraces, the upper one paved with flat stones. The south end was an inner court, the most sacred place, corresponding to the Holiest of Holies of the Jews. Here were the idols, great and small. Here was the high-priest's station. Here the gods were consulted, and their oracles made known. At the entrance to this court was the sacrificial altar of Ku.

When Aelani and Hiwa and Kaanaana and the chiefs and warriors had gathered in the temple, and Aa, grievously wounded, was brought before the altar where he had long officiated as high-priest, his proud and cruel spirit flashed forth, and he said:—"If I had won the battle I would have gone to Kohala and put every man, woman and child to the spear, save Aelani and Hiwa and Kaanaana and all of noble birth, whom I would have kept for the sacrifice; I would have made Kohala fat with slaughter; I would have drenched Ku's altar with the blood of the goddess-born. Then Ku would have had

THE SACRIFICE

more cause for rejoicing than in the sacrifice of one old man. Yet, although my bones will be put to shame, I am content, knowing that Ku's heavy wrath will fall upon my enemies, and that I shall glory in their destruction, and mock them in the other world. If Hiwa had been slain when she committed the unpardonable sin against Ku his anger might have been appeased; but now that it has been growing these sixteen years, the whole people are doomed, for they are her people and her son's. Behold I, Aa, high-priest of Ku, proclaim that his implacable wrath rests upon the whole kingdom, and shall eat up its inhabitants. My revenge is sure. Therefore I rejoice, and shall return rejoicing to the gods from whom I came!"

As the high-priest ceased speaking Kaanaana sprang towards him, crying "Aa, you lie! You invented this damning lie as a pretext for slaying the *moi wahine!* Now, in the hour of her triumph, you repeat it to ruin her before gods and men!"

Hiwa restrained him with a gesture, and said in a loud, clear voice that all might hear: "Aa does not lie. Sixteen years ago

I forgot the law which almighty Ku gave to Wakea and Papa—the law creating the sacred *tabu*, which our nation has kept age after age, and I ate of the fruit of which Ku has declared, 'In the day a woman eateth thereof she shall surely die.'"

Upon hearing this confession, the high-priest burst into a fierce, mocking laugh, and the spearmen shrank back aghast, and Kaanaana hung his head in shame and sorrow.

But Hiwa mounted the altar and stood above them, tall, straight and proud, crowned with *ilima* and *maile*, clothed with the royal robe that only a *moi* might wear and live, holding a spear in her hand.

"Sixteen years ago," she said, "I committed the unpardonable sin, and now the hour of my atonement has come. Ku spared my life. Kneeling under the rainbow, beside my new-born babe, I confessed my sin to him, and bound myself by an irrevocable vow that, if he would let me train the boy to lead the chiefs in battle for his throne, I, Hiwa, goddess-queen, with my own royal hand, would shed my sacred blood upon his altar. Ku heard the vow, and answered me with thunder from the mountains. He has kept faith with me. Now I must keep faith with him, or else his heavy wrath will fall on all I love, on all who follow me. Therefore, to save my son, Aelani, The Pledge from Heaven, to save his father, my lover, Kaanaana, who is a thousand times dearer to me than life, to save my people, whom I would not have destroyed, I keep my oath and lift the curse of Ku."

With a swift stroke she buried the spear in her own heart.

Kaanaana leaped upon the altar, crying: "Eternal Ku, although I am not goddess-born, I am a great noble. Accept my life also in atonement for her sin!" He stabbed himself, and, falling on Hiwa, died kissing her dead lips.

Then Laamaikahiki, wild with grief and rage, thrust Aa through the throat. So the high-priest died a pig's death, and his bones were put to shame.

Hiwa's bones and Kaanaana's were hidden in a cave, at dead of night, by Aelani himself, for he would not intrust this pious duty to meaner hands, that touch of mortal might not profane them so long as the world should endure. Hiwa had made such atonement, lifting Ku's curse from all the people, that they revered her memory and worshipped her as a goddess even as if she had not committed that great sin.

Aloha, Hiwa! She was nobler than a goddess-queen, for she was one of God's noblest creatures — a noble woman. Her frailties were those of human nature and of the remote and barbarous land in which she lived. Her virtues were those of a brave, generous, and lovable people.

Aloha, Hiwa! *Aloha, nui!*

GLOSSARY

The spelling of Hawaiian words is in the main phonetic, according to what is known as the continental method, with the limitation that there are only twelve letters, instead of twenty-six, in the alphabet. Hiwa, for example, is pronounced, approximately, Hē-vä, and Aelani, I-lä'-ny.

The following rules for pronunciation are taken from Prof. William D. Alexander's *Brief History of the Hawaiian People:*

The original Hawaiian alphabet, adopted by the first missionaries, contained but twelve letters, five of which were vowels, and seven consonants, viz.: $a, e, i\ o, u, h, k, l, m, n, p$, and w. The number of distinct sounds are about sixteen.

No distinction was formerly made between the sounds of k and t, or between those of l and r. In poetry, however, the sound of t was preferred to that of k. The letter w generally sounds like v between the penult and the final syllable of a word.

A is sounded as in father, e as in they, i as in marine, o as in note, u as in rule, or as oo in moon.

Ai, when sounded as a dipthong, resembles the English *ay*, and *au*, the English *ou* in *loud*.

Besides the sounds mentioned above, there is in many words a guttural break between two vowels, which is represented by an apostrophe in a few common words, to distinguish their meaning, as Kina'u.

Every word and every syllable must end in a vowel, and no two consonants occur without a vowel sound between them.

The accent of about five-sixths of the words in the language is on the penult. A few of the proper names are accented on the final syllable, as Paki', Kiwalao' and Namakeha'.

A<small>A</small>—the word has a variety of meanings, among which are a spiteful person, a raging flame, a rock of rough broken lava.

A<small>E</small>, <small>KEIKE</small>—yes, child.

A<small>ELANI</small>—the pledge from heaven, a promise from the skies. Lani, heavenly, heaven-born, is a common termination of the names of Hawaiian men and women, especially those of exalted rank.

A<small>HUPUAA</small>—a large tract of land under the control of a single person, a lordship.

A<small>IALO</small>—those who eat at the king's court.

A<small>KELA</small>—a berry much like the American raspberry.

A<small>LII-NIAUPIO, TABU MOI WAHINE</small>—freely translated, goddess-queen, a female sovereign of divine or semi-divine lineage, unapproachable, sacred, absolute.

GLOSSARY

Aloha—Aloha, more appropriately, perhaps, than any other one word, may be taken as typical of the Hawaiian race. It is the first native word the stranger learns, the common salutation on the street, and the last he hears at parting. It signifies kindly feeling, good-will. It is also used to express love.

Aloha nui—great good-will.

Au-we—an exclamation of sorrow, a wailing cry, alas.

Awa—an intoxicating liquor made from the roots of a plant of the same name. It is very stupefying, and, when drank to excess, causes the skin to turn a dirty-brown color, and to crack and flake off.

Eaeakai—the word, sometimes used as a proper noun, means, covered with the spray of the sea.

E moe o—the customary exclamation or command to lie prostrate on the approach of royalty.

Haleakala—the House of the Sun, an extinct volcano ten thousand feet high on the Island of Maui. Its crater, over thirty miles in circumference and two thousand feet deep, is the largest in the world.

Hamakua—the name of a district in the northern part of the Island of Hawaii.

Haole—a foreigner. The term is applied to white persons, whether of Hawaiian or foreign birth, and is not often used in speaking of Asiatics.

Hawaii—the large island, twice the size of all the others combined, from which the group takes it name. It is the second in industrial and commercial importance, and probably the first in undeveloped resources.

Heiau—a temple.

Hilo—the name of two districts, North and South Hilo, on the northeastern side of the Island of Hawaii and of the chief town of the island; also of the first night in which the new moon can be seen, as it is like a twisted thread (from the verb to twist, to spin, to turn). The new moon, a crescent, indicates the outline of Hilo Bay.

Hiwa—the precious one.

Hula hula—a dance, dancers, dancing, and music. The Hawaiian hula is not necessarily immodest, but certain lascivious hulas have won a world-wide and unenviable notoriety.

Ihe—a war-club.

Ii—a word that has a variety of meanings, among which are: a selfish person, a cruel person, a sour person, a collection of small things. It is often used as a proper noun, as is also the single vowel, I. Repeated three times it forms another word—iii.

Ilima—a shrub which bears beautiful green and yellow flowers; also, the flowers.

Iiwi—a small red bird.

Kaanaana—the name of a man or woman, quite common.

GLOSSARY

Kahiki—foreign parts.

Kahlooawe—one of the smaller islands.

Kahuna—a witch-doctor or sorcerer; also, at the present time, a native quack.

Kanaka-wale—a landless freeman.

Kanaloa—one of the gods, Kane's younger brother.

Kane—a male, applied equally to human beings and animals; also, the name of one of the great gods.

Kanehoalani—the god of the sky.

Kanehulikoa—the god of the sea.

Kaukihi—a small boat, a single dug-out.

Keike—a child.

Kihei—a mantle or cloak.

Kini akua—elves.

Koa—a hard wood in great demand on account of the beautiful finish which it takes.

Kohala—North and South Kohala, the two northern districts in the Island of Hawaii.

Konouiki—a great landholder under the *moi*, virtually a feudal lord.

Ku—the name of the fiercest and most cruel of the ancient gods.

Kukailimoke—the god of war.

Kukuihaele—the high land adjoining the southeast of Waipio Valley.

Kuleana—a small holding of land.

Kupua—a demi-god.

Lanai—the name of one of the smaller islands,

literally, The Hump, from its shape; the name is applied to a veranda.

LAWALU—fish or meat wrapped in *ti* leaves, and cooked on coals or hot stones.

LEI—a wreath.

LILII—usually spelled Liilii, little one, small, often added to a name to indicate youth, or as a term of affection.

LOLO—idiotic, a fool.

LONO—the mildest and most benevolent of the Hawaiian deities. The tradition was that he taught peace and good-will, and inaugurated a golden age, and that, when he went away, he promised to return some time. When Captain Cook discovered the islands in 1778 the natives welcomed him as the long-expected Lono.

MAILE—a beautiful dark green odoriferous vine, *alyxia olive-formia*.

MAKAI—towards the sea. In the Hawaiian Islands one rarely hears the words north, south, east or west, in any reference to locality or direction. It is *makai*, towards the sea, *mauka*, away from the sea, or to windward, or to leeward, or the direction is designated by another place, as, for example, Chicago is New York of the Rocky Mountains, and Denver is San Francisco of St. Paul.

MALO—the loin-cloth formerly worn by men.

MAMO—a small bird with yellow feathers, formerly sacred to royalty. Hence a garment made of its yellow feathers. The bird is nearly or quite

GLOSSARY

extinct, and the ancient robes that have been preserved have fabulous values.

MANAO—what one thinks or advises, an opinion.

MANOA—the name of a beautiful valley in the suburbs of Honolulu; also, of an ancient or legendary princess.

MAUNA KEA—the White Mountain, from the snow that covers its summit a great part of the year. It is 13,805 feet in height.

MAUNA LOA—the Long Mountain, a great volcano, 13,675 feet high. The last eruption was in July, 1899.

MELE—a poem, a song, a hymn, a chant; in particular, the epics of the race, committed to memory and transmitted from generation to generation. Some of these epics are supposed to be hundreds of years old, and are almost as unlike modern Hawaiian as Chaucer is unlike modern English.

MILU—the god of the lower world.

MOI—a sovereign in whom is supreme authority, applied to gods and monarchs descended from the gods; but the title was continued during the half century and more that the Hawaiian government was a constitutional monarchy.

MOKUHALII—the name of the god of sharks. On Hawaii, he was known as Ukanipo.

NEWA—a feather-helmet.

NIHO PALAOA—a whale-tooth ornament worn only by persons of high rank.

HIWA

NIULII—the southeast corner of North Kohala, adjoining the Hamakua mountains.

OHELO—a reddish-brown berry similar to the whortleberry.

OHIA—a deciduous fruit, something like an apple, but less nutritious and more juicy.

OLONA—a native shrub with the qualities of hemp or flax.

OO—a small black bird with tufts of yellow feathers, sacred like the *mamo*.

PAPA—a goddess, wife of Wakea.

PAPAAKAHI—the first of all, the highest in rank.

PAU—stop, hold your tongue, that is all, the end.

PAU—the ordinary female garment of ancient times, *tapa* cloth wound round the waist, and reaching to the knees.

PELE—the goddess of volcanoes.

POHA—a berry from which a delicious jam is made.

POI—a paste made from *taro*. It is to Hawaiians what wheat is to Europeans, and rice to Chinamen.

POLOLU—a short spear.

PUKA—a hole, an entrance.

PUNA—the name of a district at the eastern end of the Island of Hawaii.

PUUHONUA—a city of refuge.

TABU—prohibited, forbidden, sacred, devoted to the gods, the *moi* or the chiefs. The *tabu*, also

GLOSSARY

spelled *kapu*, was the controlling feature of the ancient religion. It was oppressive to the last degree, and was mercilessly enforced by superstitious terror and the death penalty. After the discovery by Captain Cook, it gradually lost its hold on rulers, priesthood, and people. It was officially abolished in 1819, a few months before the arrival of the first missionaries.

TAPA—a cloth made from the beaten bark of the wauki, or mamaki, or paper-mulberry or other trees; hence, any garment made of *tapa*. Also spelled *kapa*.

"Ua mau ke ea o ka aina i ka pono."
(The life of the land is preserved by righteousness.) The national motto inscribed on the Hawaiian coat-of-arms. It is, of course, of comparatively recent date, and of missionary origin.

"Ue, ue! Ua make kuu alii!
Ue, ue! Ua make kuu alii!"
(Alas! Dead is the chief!
Alas! Dead is the chief!)
The first lines of an old dirge.

UKEKE—a rude musical instrument, something like a guitar.

UKANIPO—one of the names of the shark-god.

ULUA—an excellent table-fish, very active.

UMU—an oven, a place for baking food.

WAHINE—a female; the word used to designate the female sex whether of human beings or animals.

HIWA

Waipio—the arc of water, the name of a picturesque and beautiful valley among the Hamakua mountains, derived from the waterfall. It was a royal residence for centuries, and has been the scene of many battles.

Wakea—a god prominent in Hawaiian mythology, the husband of Papa. According to some legends, Wakea and Papa were the parents of the human race, or, at least, the Polynesian branch of it; according to other legends their descendants were divine, demi-gods and demi-goddesses, like Hiwa.

Wiki wiki—hurry up.

PAU

Made in the USA
Lexington, KY
27 February 2010